Story Time with Signs & Rhymes

Shape Detective
Sign Language for Shapes

by Dawn Babb Prochovnic
illustrated by Stephanie Bauer

Content Consultant:
Lora Heller, MS, MT-BC, LCAT
and Founding Director of Baby Fingers LLC

magic Wagon

visit us at www.abdopublishing.com

For Katia and Nikko, who fill my heart with mystery and magic—DP
For kutest Kevin!—SB

Printed in the United States of America, North Mankato, Minnesota.
102011
012012
♻ This book contains at least 10% recycled materials.

Written by Dawn Babb Prochovnic
Illustrations by Stephanie Bauer
Edited by Stephanie Hedlund and Rochelle Baltzer
Cover and interior layout and design by Neil Klinepier

Story Time with Signs & Rhymes provides an introduction to ASL vocabulary through stories that are written and structured in English. ASL is a separate language with its own structure. Just as there are personal and regional variations in spoken and written languages, there are similar variations in sign language.

Library of Congress Cataloging-in-Publication Data

Prochovnic, Dawn Babb.
  Shape detective : sign language for shapes / by Dawn Babb Prochovnic ; illustrated by Stephanie Bauer.
    p. cm. -- (Story time with signs & rhymes)
  Summary: Playful images and simple rhymes introduce the American Sign Language signs for shapes.
  ISBN 978-1-61641-840-3
  1. Shapes--Juvenile fiction. 2. Animals--Juvenile fiction. 3. American Sign Language--Juvenile fiction. 4. Stories in rhyme. [1. Stories in rhyme. 2. Shape--Fiction. 3. Animals--Fiction. 4. Sign language--Fiction.] I. Bauer, Stephanie, ill. II. Title. III. Series: Story time with signs & rhymes.
  PZ10.4.P76Sh 2012
  [E]--dc23
                                2011027075

Alphabet Handshapes

American Sign Language (ASL) is a visual language that uses handshapes, movements, and facial expressions. Sometimes people spell English words by making the handshape for each letter in the word they want to sign. This is called fingerspelling. The pictures below show the handshapes for each letter in the manual alphabet.

Are you a **shape** detective? Do you like to search for shapes?

shape

Do you see a bowl of **ovals** when you munch a bunch of grapes?

oval

Can you spy a golden **circle** in the sunny summer sky?

circle

Is your kite a pointy **rhombus**, floating, spinning, flying high?

rhombus

Do you holler, "Catch the **sphere**!" if you're playing with a ball?

sphere

Does your bucket form the cubes for your sturdy castle wall?

cube

Do you notice **slopes** and angles as a ship is set to sail?

slope

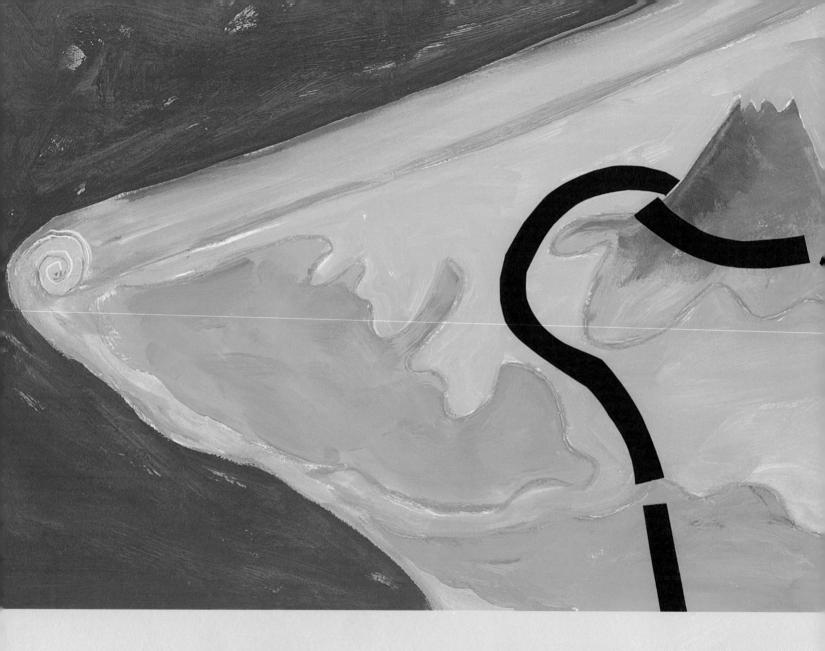

When you follow **lines** and curves, do you find a hidden trail?

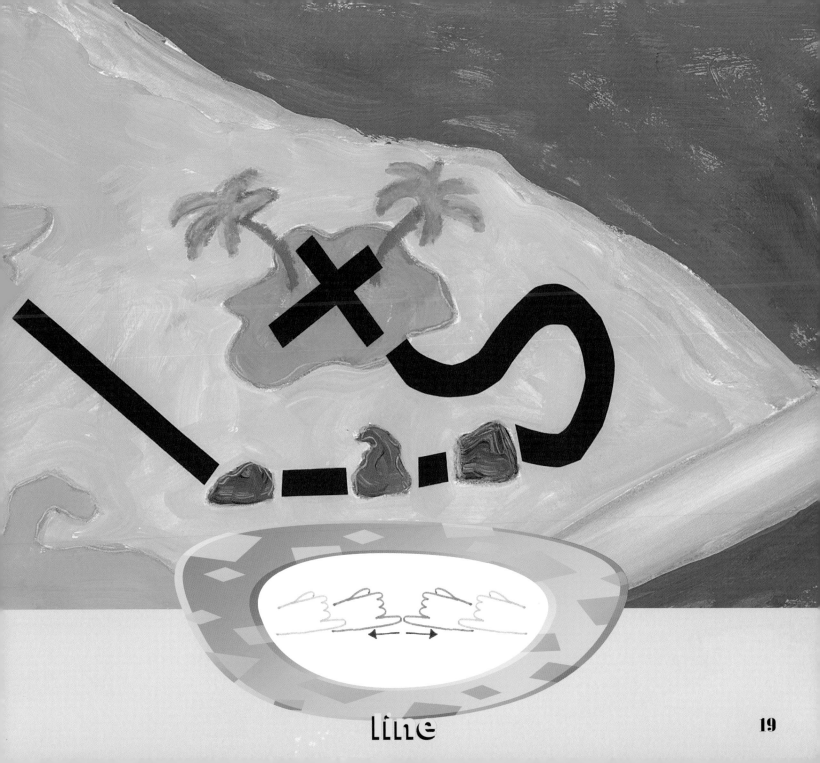

line

If you nibble on a cracker, do you crunch a salty **square**?

square

Do you measure all the pieces if your brother wants to share?

measure

Can you name the empty space where you've lost a wiggly tooth?

rectangle

Then you're a shape **detective**, a geometric sleuth!

detective

American Sign Language Glossary

circle: Hold your hand with your pointer finger pointing out and your palm facing down. Now draw the shape of a circle in the air.

cube: *Use the sign for box* by holding one hand in front of the other and both palms facing in. Your fingertips should be pointing in opposite directions. Now move your hands apart so your palms are facing each other and your fingertips are pointing away from you. It should look like you are using the palms of your hands to outline the shape of a cube or box.

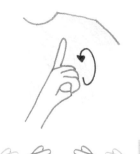

detective: Hold your right "D Hand" near the left side of your chest, and make a couple of small circles in the air. It should look like you are showing where a police detective wears a badge.

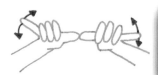

line: Make "I" handshapes with both of your hands, but position your hands sideways so your palms are facing toward you and the tips of your pinkie fingers are touching each other. Now move your hands away from each other in one straight motion. It should look like you are showing the shape of a straight line.

measure: Hold your "Y Hands" in front of you with the tips of your thumbs touching and your palms facing down. Keep your thumbs together and twist your hands a couple of times so your pinkie fingers move up and down in an alternating motion.

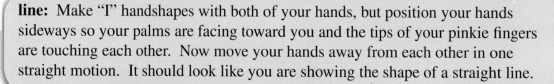

oval: Fingerspell, O-V-A-L.

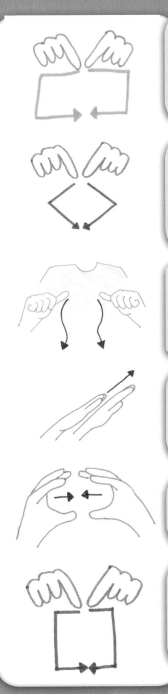

rectangle: Hold your pointer fingers in front of you with the sides of your fingertips touching and your palms facing slightly down. Now move your hands away from each other, then down, then toward each other until the sides of the fingertips are touching again. It should look like you are using your pointer fingers to draw the shape of a rectangle in the air.

rhombus: Hold your pointer fingers in front of you with the sides of your fingertips touching and your palms facing slightly down. Now move your hands away from each other at an angle, then down and back toward each other until the sides of the fingertips are touching again. It should look like you are using your pointer fingers to draw the shape of a rhombus in the air.

shape: Hold your "Ten Hands" in front of you with your palms facing out and your thumbs pointing slightly up and toward each other. Now bring your hands down toward your waist in a wavy, curvy motion. It should look like you are outlining the shape of something curvy.

slope: Hold your hands in front of you with the right hand on top of the left and both of your palms facing down. Your fingertips should point forward. Now move your right hand up and away from your left hand in a diagonal direction. It should look like you are showing the slope of a hill or mountain.

sphere: Hold your curved hands in front of you with your palms facing each other and your fingertips almost touching. Now tap your fingertips together a couple of times. It should look like you are making the round shape of a ball.

square: Hold your pointer fingers in front of you with the sides of your fingertips touching and your palms facing slightly down. Now move your hands away from each other, then down, then toward each other, until the sides of the fingertips are touching again. It should look like you are using your pointer fingers to draw the shape of a square in the air.

Fun Facts about ASL

If you know you are going to repeat a fingerspelled word during a conversation or story, you can fingerspell it the first time, then show a hand motion that you can use when the word comes up again. For example, you can fingerspell O-V-A-L, then use your pointer finger to make the shape of an oval in the air. This shows your signing partner that you mean "oval" the next time you make that hand motion.

Most sign language dictionaries describe how a sign looks for a right-handed signer. If you are left-handed, you would modify the instructions so the signs feel more comfortable to you. For example, to sign *detective*, a left-handed signer would circle their left "D Hand" near the right side of their chest.

Some signs use the handshape for the letter a word begins with to make the sign. These are called initialized signs. One example of an initialized sign is the word *detective*!

Signing Activities

X Marks the Spot: This is a fun game for partners. Choose someone to be a mapmaker and someone to be a detective. The mapmaker looks around the room and selects an object for the detective to find. The mapmaker draws a map of the room and puts an "X" at the spot where the object is located. The map should include at least three shape clues to help the detective find the object. For example, if the object is a ball, a circle should be drawn around the "X" to show the detective that the object they are trying to find is round. If the detective takes more than five minutes to find the object, the mapmaker can use signs and fingerspelling to give clues. Change roles once the detective finds the object.

Speed Signing: List the words from the glossary on a poster, then get a group together and sit in a semicircle. Choose someone to be the leader. The leader points to one word on the poster, and the other players must make the sign for that word. The leader points to another word on the poster, and the other players must make the sign for the new word. See how fast the leader can point to new words for the other players to sign before everyone starts giggling!

Additional Resources

Further Reading

Coleman, Rachel. *Once Upon a Time* (Signing Time DVD, Series 2, Volume 11). Two Little Hands Productions, 2008.

Edge, Nellie. *ABC Phonics: Sing, Sign, and Read!* Northlight Communications, 2010.

Heller, Lora. *Sign Language for Kids*. Sterling, 2004.

Valli, Clayton. *The Gallaudet Dictionary of American Sign Language*. Gallaudet University Press, 2005.

Web Sites

To learn more about ASL, visit ABDO Group online at **www.abdopublishing.com**. Web sites about ASL are featured on our Book Links page. These links are routinely monitored and updated to provide the most current information available.